FIRST SNOW

Emily Arnold McCully

W9-DBC-814

HarperTrophy
A Division of HarperCollinsPublishers

First Snow
Copyright © 1985 by Emily Arnold McCully
Printed in Mexico. All rights reserved.
Library of Congress Cataloging-in-Publication Data
McCully, Emily Arnold.   First snow.
  Summary: A timid little mouse discovers the thrill of sledding in the first snow of the winter.
  1. Children's stories, American. [1. Mice—Fiction. 2. Snow—Fiction.
3. Stories without words] I. Title.   "A Harper Trophy book"
PZ7.M478415Fi 1985   [E]   84-43244   ISBN 0-06-443181-9 (pbk.)
ISBN 0-06-024128-4. — ISBN 0-06-024129-2 (lib. bdg.)   First Harper Trophy edition, 1988